FREDDY YETI
GETS A PET

Freddie Yeti's mind was set on getting a pet.

Freddie Yeti Gets a Pet

Copyright © 2021 by Annika Jeras.

All rights reserved. No part of this book may be reproduced in any form or by any electronic or mechanical means, including information storage and retrieval systems, without permission in writing from the publisher, except by a reviewer who may quote brief passages in a review.

Whether it was a cat, a dog, a hamster, or a bird...

every one of Freddie's friends had a pet, and Freddie felt left out.

Freddie tried to play pretend with his stuffed animals. Even though he loved them very much, they weren't the same as a real-life pet...

...no matter how hard Freddie tried to train them!

Freddie thought it was about time he got his own pet. After all, he was 6 years old. He was a big kid now.

If he could tie his own shoes, he could certainly handle the responsibility of having a pet.

After a lot of convincing, Mama Yeti finally gave in. Freddie could have a pet!

But...Mama Yeti would only agree to getting Freddie a fish.

Freddie was hoping for something fluffier or more active, but he would just have to make do.

Freddie named his new fish friend Blue, since, of course, he was a blue fish.

Freddie couldn't take Blue for a walk or pet him.

He couldn't play fetch with Blue or teach him to shake. What was Freddie supposed to do with a pet that couldn't do anything?

That night, the neighbor's dog woke Freddie up.

Later at school, Freddie's class learned about different pets. Freddie learned about all the things other pets need, like space to run around, baths, and lots of exercise!

Things Pets Need:
1. Food
2. Water
3. Space
4. Exercise
5. Toys
6. Baths
7. Grooming
8. Vet Visits

Slowly but surely, Freddie started to like Blue more and more. He was quiet, didn't take up much space, never needed a bath...

...and he was a really good listener!

Freddie had even started to figure out fun ways to spend time with Blue. He couldn't take him on a walk or play fetch with him, but Blue was getting pretty good at Hide and Seek...

...and was great at tic-tac-toe!

While at first Freddie thought he wanted a pet like a dog or cat, he realized Blue was actually the perfect pet for him!

It turned out fish could be just as fun to have as other pets!

Freddie was so glad to have Blue, not only as his pet, but also as his friend.

Freddie couldn't wait to see what other memories they would make together.

Made in the USA
Coppell, TX
08 December 2021